Karen's Telephone Trouble

Other books by
Ann M. Martin

Leo the Magnificat
Rachel Parker, Kindergarten Show-off
Eleven Kids, One Summer
Ma and Pa Dracula
Yours Turly, Shirley
Ten Kids, No Pets
With You and Without You
Me and Katie (the Pest)
Stage Fright
Inside Out
Bummer Summer

THE BABY-SITTERS CLUB series
THE BABY-SITTERS CLUB mysteries
THE KIDS IN MS. COLMAN'S CLASS series
BABY-SITTERS LITTLE SISTER series
(see inside book covers for a complete listing)

Little Sister

Karen's Telephone Trouble
Ann M. Martin

Illustrations by Susan Tang

A
LITTLE APPLE
PAPERBACK

SCHOLASTIC INC.
New York Toronto London Auckland Sydney

No part of this publication may be reproduced in whole or in part, or stored in a retrieval system, or transmitted in any form or by any means, electronic, mechanical, photocopying, recording, or otherwise, without written permission of the publisher. For information regarding permission, write to Scholastic Inc., 555 Broadway, New York, NY 10012.

ISBN 0-590-69194-5

12 11 10 9 8 7 6 5 4 3 2 1   7 8 9/9 0 1 2/0

Printed in the U.S.A.   40

First Scholastic printing, June 1997

The author gratefully acknowledges
Stephanie Calmenson
for her help
with this book.

Karen's Telephone Trouble

Want to Hear a Joke?

Tweet-tweet! Tweet-tweet! Birds were singing outside my window. Sunlight was pouring in. Birds. Sun. I opened my eyes.

It was Saturday morning. That meant no school. It was June. That meant warm weather. I popped out of bed. I did not want to waste any time starting the day.

I heard voices coming from the kitchen. I washed, dressed, and ran downstairs.

"Good morning, everybody!" I said.

"Good morning, sweetheart," said Daddy.

In case you are wondering, my name is

not really sweetheart. It is Karen. Karen Brewer. I am seven years old. I have blonde hair, blue eyes, and a bunch of freckles. I wear glasses. I have two pairs. I wear the blue pair for reading and the pink pair the rest of the time.

Dingdong.

"I will get it!" I said.

Hannie was at our front door. She is one of my two best friends.

"I am going to ride my bike. Want to ride with me?" she asked.

"I got up late today," I said. "I have not even had my breakfast yet. I will meet you later, okay?"

"Okay, see you," Hannie replied.

I went back to the kitchen and poured a bowl of Krispy Krunchy cereal. It is my favorite kind.

"I am going over to Stacey's house," said Kristy. " 'Bye, everyone."

Kristy is my thirteen-year-old stepsister. She and her friends have their own baby-sitting business. Kristy is the president.

2

"Come on, Charlie," said Sam. "I told the guys we would meet them on the basketball court around nine."

Sam and Charlie are my stepbrothers. They are so old they are in high school.

"I will not be home for lunch," called David Michael on his way out the door. David Michael is my seven-year-old stepbrother. He was going to spend the day with his friend Linny, who is Hannie's older brother.

Elizabeth and Nannie decided to take Emily and Andrew to the park. (Elizabeth is my stepmother. Nannie is my stepgrandmother. Emily is my two-and-a-half-year-old sister. Andrew is my four-year-old brother.)

That left just me and Daddy. Then Daddy said, "I hate to leave you eating alone, but I have some important work to do this morning." (Daddy's office is at home.)

"That is okay," I said. "I have a phone call to make anyway."

While I was eating my cereal, I had

thought of a gigundoly funny joke I wanted to tell my classmates. We have been trading jokes all week. I dialed Nancy Dawes's number. Nancy is my other best friend. Thank goodness she was home.

"Hi," I said. "Here is your joke of the morning. What kind of jokes do breakfast cereals like best?"

"I don't know," replied Nancy. "What kind?"

"Corny ones!" I cried.

Nancy thought this was hysterical.

"I will call Terri and Tammy," she said.

Terri and Tammy are two of our classmates. (They are twins.) I knew that by the end of the day everyone in our class would have heard my joke.

Dingdong. I ran to the door. Melody Korman was there. She is seven and lives across the street. She looked like she could not wait to hear my joke. So I told it to her.

Melody thought it was very funny. We went outside to tell it to the other kids. All

4

day long I went in and out of the house making phone calls. I had to be sure everyone heard my joke. When I was sure all my classmates had heard it, I called my little-house family.

Wait. I did not tell you yet that I have two families. Really, I do. I am not joking!

The Real and True Story of My Two Families

Here is the story of how I got two families. It started when I was little. Back then I lived in one big house with Mommy, Daddy, and Andrew. Then Mommy and Daddy started to fight a lot. It seemed they just could not get along.

Mommy and Daddy explained to Andrew and me that they love us very much. But they could not live together happily anymore. So they got divorced.

Andrew and I moved with Mommy to a little house not too far away in Stoneybrook,

Connecticut. Then she met a man named Seth and they got married. Now Seth is my stepfather. So the people at the little house are Mommy, Seth, Andrew, and me. There are pets, too. They are Midgie, Seth's dog; Rocky, Seth's cat; Emily Junior, my pet rat; and Bob, Andrew's hermit crab.

Daddy stayed at the big house after the divorce. (It is the house he grew up in.) Then he met a woman named Elizabeth. Daddy and Elizabeth got married and that is how Elizabeth became my stepmother. My three stepbrothers and my stepsister, Kristy, are Elizabeth's kids.

My other sister, Emily, is adopted. She came to us from a faraway country called Vietnam. (I named my pet rat after Emily because I love her so much.) Then Nannie moved in to help out with Emily, but really she helps us all.

There are pets at the big house, too. They are Shannon, David Michael's big Bernese mountain dog puppy; Boo-Boo, Daddy's cranky old cat; Crystal Light the Second, my goldfish; and Goldfishie, Andrew's gorilla (just joking). Also, Emily Junior and Bob live at the big house whenever Andrew and I do. We switch houses every month — one month we live at the little house, the next month we live at the big house.

I have special names for my brother and me. I call us Andrew Two-Two and Karen Two-Two. (I thought up those names after my teacher read a book to our class. It was called *Jacob Two-Two Meets the Hooded Fang*.) I call us those names because we have two of so many things. We have two families, two cats, and two dogs. We have two sets of toys and clothes and books — one set at each house. That makes going back and forth easier. I have two bicycles. Andrew has two tricycles. I have two stuffed cats. (Goosie lives at the little house. Moosie lives at the big house.) And you already know that I have two best friends. Nancy lives next door to the little house. Hannie lives across the street and one house down from the big house. Nancy and Hannie and I call ourselves the Three Musketeers. That is because we like to do everything together. We are even in the same second-grade class at Stoneybrook Academy.

And that is the real and true story of my two houses. By the way, do you know which animal can jump higher than a house? No? I'll tell you. Any animal. Houses don't jump. (Another joke. Ha!)

3

Joke of the Day

By Tuesday afternoon my cereal joke had turned soggy. But that was no problem. I had a funny new joke every day. The kids in my class were very impressed. They did not know the secret about where I got my jokes. Only Hannie and Nancy knew.

I had read an advertisement in our newspaper for a joke-a-day phone service. Every afternoon when I got home from school, I called it: 1-900-555-HAHA.

"Hello, joke lovers! Get ready for your

joke of the day!" said the voice on the other end of the phone. "Did you hear about the actress who sat in the bathtub all afternoon? She wanted to be in a soap opera! Hee-ha-ha!" *Click.*

I called Hannie and told her the joke. She called Nancy. The joke was on its way to everyone in my class.

I was thinking about whom to call next when I noticed another 900 number in the paper. It was the Horoscope Hotline. I called the number and followed the instructions. A friendly voice talked about the moon and the stars. Then the good part came.

"You will have a rewarding day tomorrow," said the voice.

This was good news. We were going to have a spelling bee at school. Maybe I would win.

I called the number again to get Hannie's horoscope. Her horoscope said she had to be extra careful to avoid accidents. I decided to call Hannie right away to warn her.

"Can I use the phone?" asked Charlie.

"Can you wait until I make one more call?" I asked.

"Never mind. I am going downtown. I will call from there," said Charlie.

I called Hannie, then I called the 900 number again to get Nancy's horoscope. She was going to come into some money in the near future. I called Nancy to tell her the good news.

"Excuse me, Karen, but you are hogging the phone. I need to make a call. It is about my homework," said Kristy.

That sounded important. I let Kristy use the phone. While I was waiting for her to finish, I heard about a phone-in contest.

"Details right after this song," said the announcer on the radio.

I waved my arms at Kristy and mouthed the words "Please hurry up!" I tapped my foot and stared at her until she hung up.

"Ready, listeners? Our ninth caller wins an all-expenses-paid trip to Disney World!"

said the voice on the radio. "And here is the number to call."

I dialed the number fast. It was busy. I pressed the redial button. Still busy. I pressed it again. *Ring, ring.* Yippee!

"Hello, thank you for calling Radio One-one-one," said a voice.

"Am I the ninth caller?" I asked.

"I am sorry," said the voice. "You are our twelfth caller. But we thank you for listening to our station."

"You are welcome," I replied. "Would you like to hear a funny joke?" I asked.

"Sure," said the voice.

I told her my soap-opera joke. She laughed. She asked if I listened to the radio station often. Just then I heard a click on the line.

"Um, could you please hold on a minute? We have call waiting and someone is trying to get through," I explained.

I took the other call. It was a friend of Charlie's. She gave me a long message. I wrote it down as fast as I could. When I got back on the other line, the person from the radio station was gone. Boo.

When Charlie came home, I gave him the message, but he could not read it. It was too sloppy.

"Can you tell me what it says?" he asked.

"Let's see. Your friend said to meet her somewhere. Only I cannot read what I wrote. She is going to be there soon. Only I cannot remember the time," I said.

"That is some message, Karen," said Charlie. "I better call her myself."

Uh-oh. His friend had said she was leaving right away and could not be reached. I decided it would be a good idea if I could not be reached either. I ran to my room to hide out.

The Phone Hogs

Hannie and Nancy came over to the big house after school on Wednesday.

"Let's call the Horoscope Hotline," I said.

I dialed the 900 number. I listened to the stuff about the moon and the stars. Then I repeated the good part to my friends.

" 'You will be the center of attention this month. Use your time wisely and well.' All right!" I said. I love being the center of attention.

After I hung up the phone, Hannie and Nancy called for their horoscopes. Hannie's said she was going to be rich by next Sunday. Nancy was going to be a famous movie star.

"Let's call the joke-a-day line," said Nancy.

Before we had a chance to make the call, the phone rang. It was Bobby Gianelli, who is in our class. He had a new joke to tell us.

"What is a vampire's favorite fruit?" he asked.

The Three Musketeers were stumped.

"Neck-tarines!" said Bobby.

This was an excellent joke. We promised to call Addie Sidney, who is also in our class, and tell it to her. She would pass the joke to someone else in our class. While I was talking to Addie, another call came in.

"Hold on, please. I will be right back," I said to Addie.

I took the other call. It was one of Nannie's friends from her bowling league. Nannie was not home and I did not have a pencil to write down the message. But that was okay. I would remember to tell her later.

I said good-bye to Nannie's friend. Then Hannie and Nancy each took turns talking to Addie.

"There is another call on the line," said Nancy. She said a quick good-bye to Addie and passed me the phone.

This time the call was for David Michael. One of his classmates had a question about their homework.

"David Michael is not home now. I will tell him to call you later," I said.

I hung up the phone. Kristy came in.

"May I use the phone, please?" she asked.

"We have several more calls to make," I said. I tried to sound important.

"Oh, all right," said Kristy. "I guess my call can wait. But hurry up, okay?"

As soon as Kristy walked away, I dialed 1-900-555-HAHA. While I was dialing, *another* call came in. But the joke-a-day line was already ringing. I did not want to dial the whole 900 number again. I ignored the other call.

"Hello, jokesters! How is your funny bone today? Get ready for our laugh-riot joke of the day," said the voice. "Why are twin witches so confusing? Tick, tick, tick, your time is up! Because you can't tell which witch is which! Hee-ha-ha!" *Click.*

I was laughing so much when I told Hannie and Nancy the joke.

"Let's call Ricky and tell it to him. He can pass it on," said Nancy. Ricky Torres is another boy in our class.

A few phone calls later, Nannie walked through the door. She did not look happy at all.

"Have you girls been on the phone all afternoon?" she asked. "I tried calling from the supermarket to find out if we needed eggs. But no one answered the phone."

Gulp. That must have been the call I did not answer.

"Sorry," I said. "I was in the middle of an important phone call."

"It is time to make your important calls

somewhere else. You *must* let others use this phone," said Nannie.

Boo and bullfrogs. I did not want to leave the big house. I was afraid I might miss a call. But Nannie said we had no choice. So we marched across the street to Hannie's.

Big Trouble

I was on my own after school the next day. Daddy and Kristy were the only ones home and they were both busy. Daddy was in his office and Kristy was in her room.

I ate the snack Nannie had left for me. Then I headed for the phone. First I called the Horoscope Hotline. My horoscope was gigundoly interesting: Life will present you with a bouquet of flowers — but watch out for thorns. Hmm. I would have to think about that later.

I called the hotline two more times for

Hannie's and Nancy's horoscopes. Then I called my friends, but neither one answered. I made a note in my head to call them later.

It was time for me to call 1-900-555-HA-HA.

"Hello, jokesters! Here's your rib-tickling joke of the day: What time is it when five grizzly bears are chasing you? Five after one. Hee-ha-ha!" *Click.*

I wanted to share the joke with my classmates right away. I decided to call Natalie Springer first because I knew she would be home that afternoon. I was in the middle of dialing when I heard an announcement about another radio contest.

"The sixth caller to reach us and say, 'Radio One-one-one is fun, fun, fun,' will be our grand-prize winner today. You will win a visit to our New York City office and lunch at a fine restaurant in Rockefeller Center."

I punched in the number as fast as I could.

"Radio One-one-one! You are our fifth

caller," said a voice I did not recognize. I hung up and tried again. The voice said, "Radio One-one-one. I am sorry, we already have our winner."

Too bad. A trip to New York City could have been fun, fun, fun. I dialed Natalie's number.

"Hi, Natalie," I said. "It is me, Karen. Want to hear a great joke?"

"Sure," replied Natalie.

I told her the joke of the day. She did not get it. While I was explaining it to her, another call came in.

"Hang on, Natalie," I said. "I will be right back."

The call was for Kristy. It was her friend Stacey McGill. Kristy was upstairs doing her homework. I did not feel like going up to get her because Natalie was on the other line.

"Can I take a message for Kristy?" I asked.

"Thank you," said Stacey. "The message is

very important. Kristy is waiting to hear which one of us is baby-sitting at the Arnolds' tonight. I just found out that I cannot go. So please be sure you tell Kristy she must be there at six o'clock sharp. I will call the Arnolds now and let them know Kristy will be their sitter. Are you writing this down, Karen?"

"Oh, yes," I replied. I had not written down a word. But I was listening carefully.

After I said good-bye to Stacey, I returned to my conversation with Natalie. When Natalie finally understood the joke, she thought it was a riot. She promised to call and tell it to a few of our classmates. I got busy calling the others.

I reached Ricky and Bobby. Then Hannie called me. I was filling her in on her horoscope when Nannie walked in. She gave me a please-get-off-the-phone look.

"I have to go, Hannie," I said.

I did not mind. I had already made most of the calls I needed to make.

I did some homework. Then I helped Nannie fix dinner. We were having turkey burgers and salad. Yum.

After dinner I went upstairs to read. The phone rang around six-thirty. Elizabeth answered it.

"Kristy is not home right now," I heard her say.

It was quiet for a minute. Then Elizabeth said, "I am sorry you are upset, Mrs. Arnold. Kristy took a last-minute babysitting job at the Kormans'. There must have been some kind of mix-up. Kristy is very reliable. She must not have known you needed her."

Uh-oh. I had forgotten about Stacey's message. I had a feeling I was in Big Trouble.

Rule Number One

I was right about being in trouble. To begin with, Daddy and Elizabeth were angry with me.

"That was very irresponsible of you, Karen," said Daddy.

"How would you like it if someone did not give you an important message?" asked Elizabeth.

I said I would not like it very much.

Then Kristy came home from the Kormans'. When she found out what had happened, she was furious.

"I cannot believe you did this!" she said. "How could you forget an important message like that?"

Kristy called the Arnolds right away to apologize for not showing up. When she hung up the phone, she looked kind of pale.

"The Arnolds had to cancel their dinner reservations and stay home. They are very angry with me. And that is not the worst part. They say they are angry with the Baby-sitters Club. This makes our whole business look bad," said Kristy.

"I am sorry," I said. And I meant it.

Next it was Charlie's turn to be angry at me.

"I missed my friend the other day because I did not know where or when I was supposed to meet her. Thanks to you," he said.

"At least you got part of your message," said Sam. "My friend Robert told me he called yesterday and I never even found out about it."

Oops. I had forgotten about that call, too.

The only people in my family who were

not angry with me were David Michael, Andrew, and Emily.

"This problem with the messages is not the only one," said Nannie. "You have been tying up the phone way too much lately."

Elizabeth and Daddy gave each other a Look.

"It is time for some rules," said Daddy. "For the next two weeks, you may make only two phone calls per day."

"Two phone calls! But I am a very popular person," I said.

"Two weeks. Two phone calls. Time for bed," said Daddy.

I decided to quit while I was ahead.

"Good night, everyone," I said. And I went to my room.

Rule Number Two

By recess the next day, I had a plan. Daddy had said I could *make* only two phone calls. He had not said anything about how many I could *receive*. So I told my classmates to call me.

I expected the phone to ring as soon as I walked in the door. It did not.

I had a snack with Nannie, Andrew, and Emily. When Emily dumped her bowl of sliced bananas and yogurt on the floor, I slipped off to make my first call.

I dialed 1-900-555-HAHA.

"Hello, comedians! This is your joke-a-day host speaking. Are you ready for another knee-slapping funny? Here we go," said the voice. "Why did the boy bring a candy bar to the dentist? Because he was hungry? Wrong. Because he wanted a chocolate filling! Hee-ha-ha." *Click.*

I laughed. I wanted to call one of my classmates right away. But I did not want to use up another phone call. I would just have to wait for . . .

Ring, ring.

"Hello?" I said.

Nannie came out of the kitchen, followed by Andrew and Emily. Nannie looked as though she were expecting a call.

"It is for me," I said. "It is Hannie."

Nannie took Andrew and Emily out to the yard. I told Hannie the knee-slapping joke of the day.

"That is great," said Hannie. "I will call Nancy."

"Ask her to call me when you hang up," I said.

32

While I was waiting for Nancy to call, I turned on Radio 111. It was perfect timing. They were announcing their daily contest.

"Our twenty-first caller will win eleven CDs of his or her choice, plus a visit to our studio," said the announcer. "Call Radio One-one-one and win, win, win!"

I punched in the phone number. I already knew it by heart. I needed to win on my first try. I could not call back. This was my second and last call of the day.

Ring, ring.

"Hello, you are our eighteenth caller. Please try again," said the voice. Rats. The person who answered hung up quickly. I did not even have time to chat with him.

That was it. I had made my two phone calls. Now all I could do was wait for someone to call me. I looked at my watch. One minute passed. Two minutes. Two and a half . . .

Ring, ring.

"Hello?" I said.

Thank goodness it was Nancy. We talked until I heard the call waiting click.

"Hang on please, Nancy," I said. It was Ricky.

I asked Nancy to call me back later and took Ricky's call. While I was talking to Ricky, Natalie called. I said good-bye to Ricky and talked to Natalie. Then Addie called. We talked for a l-o-o-o-ong time.

I was still on the phone when Nannie came back inside. I was on the phone when Daddy came out of his office. I was on the phone when Elizabeth came home from work.

Right before dinner I saw Daddy, Elizabeth, and Nannie having a little talk. I wondered if the little talk was about me. Guess what. It was.

"You are still on the phone too much," said Daddy.

Nannie handed me a three-minute timer.

"Are we going to make soft-boiled eggs?" I asked. (Sometimes we use the timer when we are making eggs.)

34

"No. You are going to use the timer to make shorter phone calls," replied Nannie.

"These are your rules. You may make no more than two calls a day. And *all* calls must end when the sand in the hourglass runs out," said Elizabeth.

"And now it is time for supper," said Daddy.

Boo. I was starting to lose my appetite.

Caught!

The next day I figured out a way to bend the new rule just enough so I could live with it. The rule was that I could talk until the sand ran out of the hourglass. So I turned over the hourglass before the sand ran out. Again and again. That way I could talk as long as I wanted. And I did.

First Hannie called. We were on for just a minute. She wanted to tell me that she was going to the library with her dad.

Then I called 1-900-555-HAHA. That call

was short, too. "Hello, Saturday jokers. Are you digging holes in your garden today? Here's a joke for you," said the voice on the line. "How much dirt is in a hole six feet long, thirteen feet wide, and nine feet deep? Put away those calculators. The answer is none. A hole is empty! Hee-ha-ha!" *Click.*

My call to the radio station was even shorter. They announced the contest right after I hung up with the joke line.

"Our prize is a big one. Caller number eleven will win a weekend at the Heavenly Hotel at one-one-one Sixth Avenue in New York City. Come on, Radio One-one-one listeners, call, call, call!"

Oh, boy. A whole weekend in the city. I could visit my pen pal Maxie. I punched the numbers in as fast as lightning.

"Hello, you are the tenth caller. Try again!" said the voice.

Oh, no. I was already stretching the hourglass rule. And if I made another call, I would break the two-phone-call rule completely. That would be terrible. Anyway, I knew I could not call fast enough to be the eleventh caller.

I would have to try another day. One of these times I would win. I just had to.

Ring, ring.

"Hello?" I said. Hooray! It was for me. It was Ricky. We had been talking for awhile when another call came in.

"Hold on, please," I said.

The call was for Sam. I had a pad and pencil ready by the phone. I wrote down the message in my neatest writing. I made sure I could read every word. Then I went back to Ricky. He was telling me a very interesting story about his friend's cat when another call came in. I considered ignoring it. But I decided I was in enough trouble already.

"I will be right back," I said.

"I better hang up," said Ricky. "My father wants to use the phone."

I took the other call. It was a wrong number. Boo.

Ring, ring. It was for me again. This was so great! This time it was my classmate Pamela Harding. I was surprised. You see, Pamela is my best enemy. She does not call me much. But it was her turn to tell me the joke that was going around. It was the joke about the hole. I told her I was the one who had started it. We ended up having a very nice and very lo-o-ong conversation. I was just turning over the hourglass for the fourth time when Daddy and Elizabeth came in from their walk with Shannon. I had been caught!

"Hang up the phone please, Karen," said Daddy.

I told Pamela I had to go. Just then Kristy came downstairs from her room.

"Karen has been on the phone all morning long," she said. She made a meanie-mo face at me. (She was still angry at me about the baby-sitting mess.)

"This is outrageous," said Daddy. He thought for a moment. Then he said, "Starting tomorrow, you are limited to five phone calls per day. This means that you may either make or receive five calls. Each call is limited to three minutes. Period."

"And you may not make or receive any more calls today, since you have been on the phone for hours," said Elizabeth.

Ring, ring. I heard Kristy pick up and say hello.

"It is for Karen. It is Bobby Gianelli," she said.

"Please tell him we are sorry, but Karen cannot come to the phone," said Daddy.

Boo and bullfrogs.

9

Costly Calls

There was no way of getting around the rules this time. I was allowed to be on the phone just fifteen minutes a day. Not one minute more. Five calls only. And everyone in my family was keeping tabs on me.

On Sunday I used one of my calls to get 1-900-555-HAHA. It was worth it.

"Hello, Sunday jokers. Get your laughing gear ready. Here is our joke of the day!" said the voice on the phone. "What fish says, 'Meow'? Tick, tick, tick. Your time is up! The answer is a catfish! Hee-ha-ha!" *Click.*

42

I giggled. Then I noticed Shannon standing by the phone. I think she was keeping tabs on me, too.

"Are you working undercover, Shannon?" I asked.

I used my second phone call for the Horoscope Hotline. I wanted to know what my future held in store.

"Look closely at your finances in the next few weeks," said the voice.

Hmm. I was wondering what that meant when the doorbell rang. I hoped it was Hannie. She had promised to come over to play. It was.

"Hi," said Hannie. "I was going to call you this morning, but I did not want to waste any of your calls."

"Good idea," I said. "I have made two phone calls already this morning."

It was raining, so we went to my room. I told Hannie the joke of the day. Then I told her my horoscope.

"Speaking of finances, I heard someone say that calls with that nine-hundred number in them cost a lot of money," said Hannie.

Gulp.

"I did not know that. How much do they cost?" I asked.

"They are at least ninety-five cents each," replied Hannie.

"Ninety-five cents!" I repeated.

"Some of them are even a dollar ninety-five or more," said Hannie.

"So that was what my horoscope was about," I said.

I ran for my calculator. With Hannie's help I figured out how many 900 calls I had made in the last couple of weeks.

"Even if they cost only ninety-five cents apiece, that comes to over forty dollars!" I said.

"You better hope the calls do not cost a dollar ninety-five. That would come to eighty dollars!" said Hannie.

I fell back on my bed.

"What are you going to do?" asked Hannie. "As soon as the phone bill comes, your father will see all of those calls. His bill will be really high."

I thought for a minute. Then I sat up tall.

"I will have to keep him from seeing the bill until I have the money to pay him back," I said. "All I have to do is get to the bill before he does."

"How will you do that?" asked Hannie.

"I do not know yet," I replied. "But I will find a way."

Yikes!

Getting to the phone bill first was not going to be easy. The mail arrives before I get home from school, and Daddy is usually right there to get it.

But sometimes Nannie brings it in and nobody even looks at it until after supper. Other times she and Daddy forget to bring it in altogether. Then I get it on my way in from school. All I could do was hope that the bill would come on a day when I could get to it first.

On Monday morning I thought about pretending to be sick. That way I was sure to be home when the mail arrived. But I decided Daddy might get suspicious. Also I did not want to miss a day of school.

I spent the whole day worrying. In the afternoon I ran to my house from the bus stop. Hannie came with me.

"If the bill is here, I am the luckiest person in the whole world," I said.

I opened the mailbox. The mail was there. Yes!

I leafed through the bundle. Boo. I was not the luckiest person in the whole world. There was no bill.

I did the same thing on Tuesday. I ran home from the bus stop and opened the mailbox. It was empty. I listened for shouting from Daddy's office. There was none. This was a good sign.

I ran inside. The mail was waiting on the hall table unopened. Thank goodness. But there was no bill.

There was no bill on Wednesday or Thursday or Friday. Daddy still was not upset. So I knew the bill had not come.

In the meantime I stopped making 900 calls. At first I missed 1-900-555-HAHA and the Horoscope Hotline. Then I noticed that my family seemed a lot happier with me. (Except for Kristy. She was still pretty angry.) I also had more time to do other things. Such as look through the mail.

On Saturday morning Hannie and I played in my front yard. We made sure we were never more than two feet from the mailbox.

Finally I saw Mr. Venta, our mailman, coming down the street. I was so nervous, I began hopping from one foot to the other. As soon as he handed me the mail, I thanked him and started leafing through it. It was a big day for bills. There were three bills from stores, one from the electric company, one from the gas company, and one from Connecticut Bell!

"We've got it!" I said to Hannie. I stuffed the bill into my pocket.

"Let's go to your room so you can open

it," said Hannie. "I cannot wait to see how much it is."

When we were inside, I dropped the rest of the mail on the hall table. Then Hannie and I dashed up to my room and closed the door.

"This is like the Academy Awards. 'The envelope, please,' " said Hannie, giggling.

"This is nothing to joke about," I said. But I started giggling, too, because I was nervous.

I slit open the envelope. I do not know how much phone bills usually are, but this looked like a very high one to me. I got out my calculator. Hannie helped me add up the cost for all the 900 calls.

"Yikes! I owe Daddy almost forty-five dollars!" I said. "Forty-four dollars and eighty-five cents to be exact."

"Yikes is right. That is *a lot* of money," said Hannie.

Just then Elizabeth called, "Girls, would you like to come downstairs for lunch?"

I quickly hid the phone bill under some

notebooks on my desk. Then I opened my door.

"We will be right there," I replied. I turned to Hannie and whispered, "We have to act normal. We cannot let on that there is anything wrong."

"I better go home. I am not such a good actress," replied Hannie.

I said good-bye to Hannie at the door. Then I put on my most normal face and went to the kitchen for some lunch.

The First Penny

After lunch I went straight to my room. I had work to do. I took out paper and a pencil. I was going to make a list of ways to earn money.

I had to make forty-five dollars in one month. That is when the telephone company would send another bill. Daddy would not be happy when he saw how much it was. But when I handed him the money I owed him, he might not be so angry.

"Okay, Moosie," I said. "Put on your

thinking cap. Forty-five dollars is a lot of money. How can I earn it?"

Moosie gave me an idea right away. That is because he looked so messy.

I would have to brush him with one of my doll brushes. I knew Shannon needed brushing, too. David Michael does not like to do that job. "I will not charge you, Moosie," I said. "But I will charge David Michael a dime."

I wrote in big letters at the top of the page, "PET GROOMING." Next to that I wrote "10 cents." That was not much money.

"I will ask if I can feed Shannon, too," I said to Moosie. "I will feed all the pets in the big house. Ten cents a pet."

I erased "PET GROOMING." I wrote, "PET CARE."

Next I wrote, "DUSTING." Nannie always hires me to dust her room when I need money.

Wait. What if someone asked what I need the money for? I would say it was a surprise. I would not be lying, either. Everyone will get a big surprise when they see that telephone bill.

Below "DUSTING," I wrote, "HELP WITH EMILY" and "WEED DADDY'S GARDEN." Hmm. The list was getting very long. I was writing down a lot of chores. But I was not even coming close to earning forty-five dollars.

I needed a new idea. I needed an idea that would make me a lot of money.

"Who makes money, Moosie? Bankers. Presidents of big companies," I said. (I happen to know that not all presidents make a lot of money. Kristy does not make any money for being president of the Baby-sitters Club.)

I had to think hard. Who else makes money?

"I know," I said. "Famous comedians. I will be a stand-up comedian. I will entertain my family."

I took out another piece of paper and started a list of jokes. Too bad I could not call 1-900-555-HAHA for the joke of the day. Oh, well. I knew plenty of jokes already.

I wrote down a page of jokes, then went downstairs to start making money. I found my first customer. Andrew was reading in the den.

"Want to hear a joke?" I asked.

"Okay," he replied.

"That will be ten cents, please," I said.

"No way!" said Andrew. "Jokes do not cost money."

"My jokes do because they are so funny," I said.

"I will give you a penny," said Andrew.

"It is a deal," I said.

I decided a penny was better than nothing. I made believe I was the voice on the joke-of-the-day line.

"Are you ready for a rib-tickling, side-splitting joke?" I asked Andrew.

"I am ready," said Andrew.

"Here it is! How can you tell if an elephant has been in your refrigerator?" I asked.

55

"Um, the shelves are broken?" guessed Andrew.

"Nice try. But wrong answer," I said. "You know an elephant has been in your refrigerator if his footprints are in the butter. Hee-ha-ha!"

"I like my answer better," said Andrew. But he dug into his pocket and came up with my penny.

It was not much. But I was happy to have it. Now I needed only forty-four dollars and eighty-four cents.

Daddy's Call

"See you tomorrow, Hannie," I called.

I was heading into my house after school on Wednesday. I planned to go straight to my room to put on my chore clothes. (I had been getting pet hair and dust all over me every afternoon.)

On my way upstairs I passed Daddy's office. I heard him talking on the phone.

"Hello, Connecticut Bell? I would like to speak with someone in charge of billing, please," he said.

Uh-oh.

"I did not receive my bill this month. I am wondering if it was sent out," continued Daddy.

It was quiet for a minute. Then Daddy said, "You will send a copy today? Excellent. Thank you very much."

Here we go again, I thought. I would have to make sure to get the bill again before Daddy saw it. I was working hard to earn the forty-five dollars I owed him. But there was no way I could earn it all before this new copy of the bill arrived.

I ran upstairs to change my clothes. As soon as I was dressed, I went to the kitchen to join Nannie and Emily for a snack. (Andrew was at a friend's house.)

When we finished eating, Nannie said, "Would you like to watch Emily while I make dinner?"

"Sure," I replied. Watching Emily was one of my highest-paying jobs.

I took Emily into the den. She wanted me to read her a book called *Dinner at the Panda Palace*. We had read it lots of times before, so

I practically knew it by heart. Mr. Panda owns a restaurant. No matter how crowded it gets, he always makes room for hungry customers.

I wondered how much money a restaurant owner makes. Probably a lot, if the restaurant is popular like the Panda Palace. Only I did not have enough time to open a restaurant before the next phone bill arrived.

Ring, ring. Ring, ring.

I started to jump up to answer the phone. But I knew Emily would start whining if I stopped reading. So I let Nannie get it. You know what? I hardly minded at all. These days I was spending less and less time talking on the phone. I was too busy making money and worrying about the phone bill.

I read Emily the last page of the book. *"No matter how many, no matter how few, there will always be room at the Palace for you."*

Hmm. Maybe I could get a job as a waitress. I would be an excellent waitress who made a lot of money in tips. Or maybe I could be the chef. I would make delicious dishes and get a very high salary.

"Again. Read again," said Emily.

"Okay," I replied. I turned to the first page and started reading the story again. This time I was saying the words, but I was not thinking about the story. I was thinking about the phone bill. I was thinking about how to get it again before Daddy did.

It's Show Time!

On Thursday afternoon Hannie and I were on the school bus when it slowed down. It was letting a truck pull out of a space at the curb. It was our mail delivery truck!

"We have to get to my house before the truck does. Otherwise Daddy or Nannie might get the phone bill first," I said.

The mail truck stopped at a corner stop sign. Then it pulled ahead. Then the school bus had to stop at the corner. The mail truck was getting farther and farther ahead. It was heading toward my house.

"Maybe we should get out here and run," I said.

"We cannot do that," replied Hannie. "The bus driver is allowed to let us out only at the bus stop."

Oh, no! I shut my eyes. I could not stand to see the mail truck reach my house before I did. Then I felt a poke in my ribs.

"Look," said Hannie. "He is pulling over again. He has a few more stops to make before your house."

Thank goodness. The school bus passed the mail truck. It pulled into our bus stop. Hannie and I jumped off and ran down the street. We were at my house waiting when the mail truck arrived. There was no bill anyway.

"That was a close call," I said to Hannie.

"It sure was," replied Hannie. "See you tomorrow."

Friday was worse than a close call. The

mail was already inside and opened by the time I got home. Daddy joined Andrew, Emily, and me for our snack. But he did not seem one bit upset. So I knew the bill had not arrived.

When I finished my snack, I excused myself and went upstairs. I had something very important to do.

I had decided I did not need to open a restaurant to make money. I had a better idea.

I tried out my idea on Moosie. Then I practiced the rest of the afternoon. I rehearsed my idea in my head all during dinner. When my family was having dessert, I went to my room and returned with my homemade sign. I marched into the dining room.

"Forget about doing chores tonight. Forget about watching TV. It is show time!" I said.

I turned over my sign. In big letters I had written:

KAREN'S COMEDY CLUB
WHERE: THE DEN
WHEN: 7:30

TICKETS: 50 CENTS

"This is great," said Daddy. "I have had a busy week. I could use a good laugh."

"So could I," said Elizabeth. "And this is a lot cheaper than a Broadway show. The tickets are my treat."

"I will bring refreshments," said Nannie.

"Cool," I said. "See you in the den."

This was so exciting. I had almost a full house. (Kristy said she had to leave for a baby-sitting job. I do not think she would have come to my show anyway.)

I turned out all the lights except for one. I shined that one on me. Then I began my comedy routine.

"What do you get when you cross a plumber with a jeweler?" I asked.

No one knew the answer, so I told them.

"Ring around the bathtub!"

Everyone laughed. I told another.

"What is a monster's favorite breakfast cereal?" I asked. "Scream of wheat!"

I told joke after joke. My family loved the show. And at the end of the night, I had four more dollars in my pocket.

Phone Trouble

I had been lucky with the phone bill so far. But I did not want to take any extra chances. On Saturday morning I got up early and stood by the mailbox. In fact, I leaned on it.

"Karen, what are you doing?" asked Charlie. "Holding up the mailbox?"

Uh-oh. I did not want anyone getting suspicious. I had to think fast.

"I am waiting for Hannie," I replied. "This is our meeting place."

It was not a bad lie. I was not expecting

Hannie. But if she did come over, this is where I would meet her.

Charlie waved as he drove away in the Junk Bucket. (That is the name of his car.) As I watched him go down the street, I saw the mail truck turn the corner and head my way.

"Good morning," said Mr. Venta.

He handed me a bundle. I thanked him and flipped through it fast. There was less mail than usual. But that did not matter. I saw just what I was looking for. The Connecticut Bell phone bill. I stuffed the bill in my pocket. It was not a moment too soon. Daddy opened the door and came out to meet me.

"It is a beautiful morning," he said. "I think I will work in my garden for awhile. Is there anything interesting in the mail?"

"I do not think so," I replied. "Here, you look."

I handed him the bundle of mail and ran into the house.

Ring, ring.

I picked up the phone, since I was standing by it when it rang. The caller wanted to speak to Nannie. I gave Nannie the phone. Then I went upstairs and hid the second bill with the first one under the notebooks on my desk.

I was feeling good the rest of the day. I helped Daddy in the garden. I played with Hannie. I was still feeling good on Sunday. And on Monday.

Then, on Tuesday after school, something happened. Something bad.

Ring, ring.

"I will get it," said Nannie.

She was getting a lot of phone calls lately. She and her friends were making plans for a mini bowling tournament.

"Yes, I can practice tonight," said Nannie. "Why don't we meet at . . . Hello? Hello? Are you still there?"

Nannie clicked the receiver button.

"That is funny," she said. "The line went dead."

Just then Daddy walked into the kitchen. Nannie told him what happened. They looked out the window.

"It is raining hard," said Daddy. "But it is not the kind of storm that would cut off a phone line."

"Everything else seems to be working fine. So there is not a power failure," said Nannie.

They stood there looking puzzled. Then Daddy said, "You know, I never did receive my phone bill this month. I wonder if our phone service has been cut off."

"Connecticut Bell is very strict about unpaid bills," said Nannie.

"I will be back in a few minutes," said Daddy. "I am going across the street to the Papadakises' house. I want to see if they are having phone troubles, too."

I followed Daddy to the hall. He stopped and got an umbrella. I followed him outside and across the street. I was so nervous I could not even talk.

I was in big telephone trouble.

15

Karen's Confession

Daddy rang the bell at the Papadakises' house. Mr. Papadakis answered.

"Good evening, Watson," he said. "Nice to see you."

"Good evening," Daddy replied. "We are having some phone trouble over at our house. I wondered if your phones are out, too."

"No. As a matter of fact, Hannie is talking on the phone right now. Why don't you come in?" Mr. Papadakis said.

"Thank you," Daddy replied. "If you

don't mind, I will call the phone company from here."

Then Daddy started grumbling about how our service must have been cut off for nonpayment.

"And *I* called *them* to let them know the first bill never arrived," Daddy explained.

Hannie waved to me.

"I am talking to Nancy," she said.

"You are going to have to hang up, because my dad needs to use your phone. And because I am in big trouble and I may need your help," I whispered.

"I will call you back later," Hannie said to Nancy.

As soon as she hung up, Daddy went to the phone. We listened to him talk to the phone company.

"The second bill never arrived even though I requested it. And now my service has been cut off," he said. "If I come downtown right now and pay my bill, would the phone service be restored immediately?"

He listened, then nodded.

"Good. I will be there shortly," said Daddy.

He turned to Mr. Papadakis and said, "Thanks for the use of your phone. I believe I am finally going to get this phone mess cleared up."

Uh-oh, I thought.

We said our good-byes. Then I followed Daddy home. He walked into the house, picked up his car keys, then turned around and headed out again. He was grumbling about the phone company the whole time.

I went to my room to think. I knew what I needed to do. I just had to build up my courage. By the time Daddy returned, I was ready.

When he walked in the door, I was there to meet him. He did not look very happy.

"Daddy, there is something important I have to tell you," I said.

Ring, ring.

"Excuse me a minute, Karen," said

Daddy. "That is probably the phone company calling."

Daddy picked up the phone.

"Yes, our service has been restored. Thank you," said Daddy. "And were you able to check our bill?"

Daddy listened for a minute.

"So all those calls really were ours. Well, thank you again," said Daddy.

He hung up the phone and turned to me.

"You were saying you had something important to tell me. Why don't you come into my office," said Daddy.

I followed Daddy into his office. He sat down in one chair. I sat in another facing him. I took a deep breath.

"I have a confession to make," I said. "It is about the phone bill."

"I am listening," said Daddy.

"The phone company really did send you the bill. They even sent it twice. But I hid the bills before you could see them," I said.

"Why don't you tell me the story from the beginning," said Daddy.

That is what I did. I told him about the 900 calls and the money I owed him. I told him how I thought he would be less angry if I had the money to pay him back.

I talked and talked. And Daddy listened.

Karen's Punishment

The last thing I did was reach into my pocket and pull out the phone bills. I handed them to Daddy.

I could tell I was in deep, deep trouble. This did not surprise me one bit.

"Please go to your room now, Karen," said Daddy. "I will have a talk with Elizabeth when she comes home. We will decide together what to do about all this."

Elizabeth was out shopping with Nannie and Emily. They returned just before dinner.

I heard Daddy and Elizabeth talking

downstairs. But I could not make out what they were saying. A few minutes later there was a knock on my door. Daddy and Elizabeth asked to come in and sit down

"What you did was very wrong," said Daddy. "It was bad enough that you made all those expensive phone calls without permission. But to take mail and hide it is very serious. In fact, it is a crime to tamper with the mail."

Gulp.

"Am I going to go to jail?" I asked.

"No," replied Elizabeth. "We are not planning to report you to the police. But there will be a punishment."

"You may not use the phone at all for two weeks," said Daddy. "That means you may not make or take a single call. And about the money. You will have to pay me back for all the calls. That comes to forty-five dollars."

"I am trying very hard to earn the money," I said. "That is why I have been doing so many chores. And that is why I put on the show. It takes a long time to earn so much money. And Kristy will not hire me to do anything because she is still upset with me."

"You have no time limit on paying me back," said Daddy. "Just remember that you may not spend money on anything else until it *is* paid off."

I slumped down in my chair. This was bad news. No phone calls. No spending money. But Daddy and Elizabeth were not being unfair. I knew I deserved the punishment.

"Oh, well." I sighed. "I guess I better get back to doing chores and making money."

"How much have you earned so far?" asked Elizabeth.

"Seven dollars and twenty-four cents," I replied.

"That leaves you thirty-seven dollars and seventy-six cents to go," said Daddy.

I hoped I would not be old and gray by the time I earned it.

The Accident

Sunday was a quiet day at the big house. This is very unusual for a house with ten people and six pets living in it.

It started out busy. We had a noisy breakfast. Sam and Charlie made some calls then went out to meet their friends.

Daddy was puttering around. Mostly he was working on the old storm door at the back entrance of the house.

When he finished, Elizabeth reminded him they had promised to take Andrew and

David Michael downtown for new sneakers. Nannie was going with them.

"Kristy, will you please baby-sit for Karen and Emily until we get back?" asked Elizabeth.

"All right," replied Kristy.

I could tell from the look she gave me that she did not like the idea of hanging around with me. But she had no choice.

"Come on, Emily," said Kristy. "We can play in the yard."

I needed a break from my chores, so I followed them outside.

We played Ring Around the Rosie. Emily threw back her head and laughed every time we sang, "All fall down!"

We played the game about six times. Then Emily started getting silly. She was singing, "All fall up-down! Up-down!" She bounced up and down on the grass.

"All right," said Kristy. "It is nap time for Emily."

"No, no. Up-down!" called Emily.

"Not up-down. Inside," said Kristy.

Kristy walked to the back door.

"Come, Emily," I said. "I will go inside, too."

I followed Kristy. Emily followed me. Kristy turned to see if we were behind her. While she was facing us she reached out and pushed in the door.

First I heard a crash. Then I heard Kristy scream in pain. The next thing I knew, she was lying flat on the ground.

"Kristy!" I called.

Emily started crying. There was a lot of blood on Kristy's hand. There were slivers of glass all over the place. Kristy had stopped screaming and was whimpering.

"Emily, stay back!" I said.

I ran to Kristy's side and bent down. She was trying to tell me something. Her voice was weak. I put my ear near her mouth so I could hear.

"I thought Watson put a screen on the door. He must have put in glass. I did not see it," said Kristy. She was having trouble catching her breath.

"You need to be quiet now," I said.

Kristy looked pale. I thought she might faint. I had to take charge. I had to get Kristy to the hospital. There was no time to lose.

"Emily, stay right by my side," I said. "We are going to help Kristy." (Thank goodness Emily had stopped crying.)

I helped Kristy inside and sat her down on a chair in the kitchen. Then I had to do something I was not supposed to do. I had to use the phone. If I got into trouble for it, I did not care. This was an emergency. I had to call 911.

Calling 911

Kristy looked very wobbly sitting in the chair. So I made her lie down on the kitchen floor.

Next I checked to see that all the animals were in the house. When I was sure they were, I locked the doors so they could not get out. I did not want them to get cut on the broken glass.

Then I found the cordless phone and brought it into the kitchen. I held Emily by the hand so she could not wander off.

Finally I took a deep breath and pressed

911. An emergency operator answered. She asked me to tell her my name, address, and what the emergency was.

"My name is Karen Brewer," I said.

I gave her our address on McLelland Road. Then I told her what had happened to Kristy. The operator asked me a few more questions about Kristy's condition. Then she told me what to do.

I had to get a clean cloth and press it against Kristy's cut. Then I had to make sure Kristy's arm was raised. I slid Kristy over to a cabinet and leaned her arm up against it.

The operator said Kristy might be in shock from her accident. She told me to cover Kristy with a light blanket and put a pillow under her legs. She said that would help.

I had found one of Emily's dolls lying on the kitchen floor. I told Emily to take care of her doll the way I was taking care of Kristy. That kept her busy. (I thought of that plan all by myself.)

"The ambulance will be there in five

minutes," said the emergency operator. "Is everything under control?"

"Yes," I replied.

"Then I want you to run outside and hang something red over your mailbox. That way the ambulance driver can find your house more quickly."

I took Emily by the hand again. I knew she could not be left alone even for a minute. (Kristy was too weak to help if Emily got into trouble.)

I found a red sweatshirt in the hall closet. I ran outside, draped it over the mailbox, and ran back inside to Kristy.

The next thing I knew, I heard sirens wailing. Lights were flashing in our driveway. The ambulance had arrived. Half the neighborhood arrived with them. Everyone was there to help us.

Mrs. Papadakis got into the ambulance with Kristy. I squeezed Kristy's hand tight.

"You are going to be okay," I promised.

"Thanks," she said.

I took Emily across the street to Hannie's house. There was one more important thing I had to do. I had to track down Daddy and Elizabeth.

I have had a lot of practice using the phone. So I knew just what to do.

I looked in the yellow pages under "shoes." There are three stores my family likes best. I hoped they would be in one of them when I called.

"Hello, this is an emergency," I told the man in Fancy Footwear. I described my family.

"Hold on," he said. "I think they are here."

I got lucky on my first try. I heard Daddy's voice on the phone.

"Karen, what is it? Are you kids all right?" he asked.

I told him the story. He said they would go straight to the hospital.

"Karen, you have done an amazing job. Thank you," said Daddy.

I felt gigundoly proud.

Radio 111

"Hi, Kristy! How are you feeling?" I asked.

I was talking on the phone to Kristy late that afternoon. She was still in the hospital. (Daddy had taken away my phone punishment because I handled the emergency so well. But I still had to pay him back the money I owed him.)

Kristy said she was doing fine. Her cut was bad enough that she had to have stitches. And they wanted her to stay overnight so they could keep an eye on her.

Elizabeth was going to stay with her. The doctors were sure she could go home the following morning.

When I hung up the phone, Andrew came into the den.

"Look at my new sneakers," he said.

He was wearing brand-new sneakers with green trim. There were lights on the sides that blinked whenever he walked.

"Cool sneakers," I said.

"Thanks," he replied. He ran to the kitchen. I heard him say, "Hey, Charlie. Look at my new sneakers."

I was feeling kind of tired. I sat back on the couch and listened to a song I like on the radio. When the song ended, the announcer said, "Hello, Radio One-one-one listeners! We have a phone-in contest you're going to love. Our eleventh caller will win one hundred eleven dollars. That's right. One hundred eleven dollars just for listening to Radio One-one-one."

I did not wait a minute. I picked up the phone. I tried to keep my hand steady as I pressed in the numbers. I did not want to misdial.

Ring, ring.

"Congratulations, you are our eleventh caller!" said the voice on the other end.

I could not believe it.

"Is this for real?" I asked.

"It sure is," said the voice. "You are our big winner. Just give us your name and address and we will send you a check for one hundred eleven dollars!"

For the second time in one day, I gave my name and address to someone who needed it for a very good reason.

"Thank you for listening to Radio One-one-one. You should be receiving your check in a few days," said the voice.

"Thank *you*," I replied. "I can really use the money."

I ran to the kitchen. It was almost dinnertime and everyone was there.

"Guess what!" I said. I told them how I had won the contest.

"I can pay you back and I will still

have money left over," I said to Daddy.

"Karen, if anyone deserves to win a contest today, it is you," said Daddy.

He gave me a great big hug.

An E-Mail Good-bye

It was a few weeks later. June had turned into July. That meant Andrew and I were back at the little house. There was no school, but that did not stop me and my classmates from exchanging jokes.

No one's family wanted their main phone line tied up. So we came up with a new idea. We used our computers to send and receive jokes by E-mail. (We had a buddy system for anyone who did not have a computer at home.)

"Mommy, can we go to the library this afternoon?" I asked.

"Of course," replied Mommy. "I have some books I would like to return anyway."

I still had contest money left over. I could have used it to call 1-900-555-HAHA. But if I started making 900 calls, my money would be gone in no time. Anyway, I would only get one joke a day. At the library I could get hundreds of jokes for free.

When we reached the library, I went straight to the humor section. I took a book called *Pocketful of Laughs* off the shelf and opened it. I read a funny joke and laughed out loud.

"Quiet in the library, please," said the librarian.

"Sorry," I whispered.

I took another book off the shelf. This one was called *Why Did the Chicken Cross the Road?* I read another joke. This time I covered my mouth and giggled quietly to myself. I put that book on top of the first one.

The next book I found was *101 Silly Summertime Jokes*. I took book after book off the shelves, until I had ten books piled high. I carried the wobbling stack to the librarian at the desk.

"What was so funny?" she whispered.

I opened *Pocketful of Laughs* and read the joke I liked best to the librarian.

"What do you call a fish with two knees?" I whispered.

The librarian shrugged. She did not know the answer.

"A two-knee fish!" I whispered.

Guess what. The librarian laughed out loud.

"I know," she whispered. "Quiet in the library, please."

When I returned home, I sat in front of our computer so I could E-mail some jokes to my classmates.

I had looked through my books and picked out my favorite ones. I was just about to send them when I got an E-mail message. It said:

Hello, Musketeer!
Do you want to play later?
My dad will drive me to your
house. Nancy wants to come,
too.

                    Hannie

I sent back a one-word message. It was:

Yippee!

I sent the jokes to my classmates. Then I
looked through my books, and found one
last joke. This one was for Kristy.

Dear Kristy,
Q: What kind of ship never
sinks?
A: Friendship!

A few seconds later a message appeared
on my screen. Kristy was at home, and she
had answered me. This was her message:

Thanks, little sister. You
are the greatest!
And that's no joke.

L. GODWIN

About the Author

ANN M. MARTIN lives in New York City and loves animals, especially cats. She has two cats of her own, Gussie and Woody.

Other books by Ann M. Martin that you might enjoy are *Stage Fright; Me and Katie (the Pest)*; and the books in *The Baby-sitters Club* series.

Ann likes ice cream and *I Love Lucy*. And she has her own little sister, whose name is Jane.

Little Sister

Don't miss # 87

KAREN'S PONY CAMP

"The Gales will deliver Blueberry to the camp in about three weeks," said Daddy. "So he will arrive while you are still there. I am glad you thought of this solution."

"Me, too!" I said. "I cannot wait to see Blueberry at camp. It will be so special to have my very own pony there."

"Okay," said Daddy." I will call you again before you leave, to say good-bye."

"Okay. Bye, Daddy. "I hung up the phone. "Mommy, Blueberry will be at camp! I bet I will be the only camper there with her very own pony."

LITTLE APPLE™

BABY-SITTERS™
Little Sister

by Ann M. Martin,
author of The Baby-sitters Club ®

☐	MQ44300-3	#1	Karen's Witch	$2.95
☐	MQ44259-7	#2	Karen's Roller Skates	$2.95
☐	MQ44299-7	#3	Karen's Worst Day	$2.95
☐	MQ44264-3	#4	Karen's Kittycat Club	$2.95
☐	MQ44258-9	#5	Karen's School Picture	$2.95
☐	MQ44298-8	#6	Karen's Little Sister	$2.95
☐	MQ44257-0	#7	Karen's Birthday	$2.95
☐	MQ42670-2	#8	Karen's Haircut	$2.95
☐	MQ43652-X	#9	Karen's Sleepover	$2.95
☐	MQ43651-1	#10	Karen's Grandmothers	$2.95
☐	MQ43645-7	#15	Karen's in Love	$2.95
☐	MQ44823-4	#20	Karen's Carnival	$2.95
☐	MQ44824-2	#21	Karen's New Teacher	$2.95
☐	MQ44833-1	#22	Karen's Little Witch	$2.95
☐	MQ44832-3	#23	Karen's Doll	$2.95
☐	MQ44859-5	#24	Karen's School Trip	$2.95
☐	MQ44831-5	#25	Karen's Pen Pal	$2.95
☐	MQ44830-7	#26	Karen's Ducklings	$2.95
☐	MQ44829-3	#27	Karen's Big Joke	$2.95
☐	MQ44828-5	#28	Karen's Tea Party	$2.95
☐	MQ44825-0	#29	Karen's Cartwheel	$2.75
☐	MQ45645-8	#30	Karen's Kittens	$2.95
☐	MQ45646-6	#31	Karen's Bully	$2.95
☐	MQ45647-4	#32	Karen's Pumpkin Patch	$2.95
☐	MQ45648-2	#33	Karen's Secret	$2.95
☐	MQ45650-4	#34	Karen's Snow Day	$2.95
☐	MQ45652-0	#35	Karen's Doll Hospital	$2.95
☐	MQ45651-2	#36	Karen's New Friend	$2.95
☐	MQ45653-9	#37	Karen's Tuba	$2.95
☐	MQ45655-5	#38	Karen's Big Lie	$2.95
☐	MQ45654-7	#39	Karen's Wedding	$2.95
☐	MQ47040-X	#40	Karen's Newspaper	$2.95
☐	MQ47041-8	#41	Karen's School	$2.95
☐	MQ47042-6	#42	Karen's Pizza Party	$2.95
☐	MQ46912-6	#43	Karen's Toothache	$2.95
☐	MQ47043-4	#44	Karen's Big Weekend	$2.95
☐	MQ47044-2	#45	Karen's Twin	$2.95
☐	MQ47045-0	#46	Karen's Baby-sitter	$2.95
☐	MQ46913-4	#47	Karen's Kite	$2.95
☐	MQ47046-9	#48	Karen's Two Families	$2.95
☐	MQ47047-7	#49	Karen's Stepmother	$2.95
☐	MQ47048-5	#50	Karen's Lucky Penny	$2.95
☐	MQ48229-7	#51	Karen's Big Top	$2.95
☐	MQ48299-8	#52	Karen's Mermaid	$2.95
☐	MQ48300-5	#53	Karen's School Bus	$2.95
☐	MQ48301-3	#54	Karen's Candy	$2.95

More Titles... ➡